COLONEL CHABERT

HONORÉ DE BALZAC

COLONEL CHABERT

TRANSLATED BY CAROL COSMAN

A NEW DIRECTIONS BOOK

Book design by Sylvia Frezzolini Severance
Manufactured in the United States of America
New Directions Books are printed on acid-free paper.
First published as a New Directions Paperbook Original in 1997

Library of Congress Cataloging-in-Publication Data
Balzac, Honoré de, 1799–1850.
    [Colonel Chabert. English]
    Colonel Chabert / Honoré de Balzac ; translated by Carol Cosman.
        p. cm.
    ISBN 978-0-8112-1359-2
    I. Cosman, Carol. II. Title.
    PQ2163.C713 1997
    843' . 7—dc21   97-10790
                                                     CIP

New Directions Books are published for James Laughlin
by New Directions Publishing Corporation,
80 Eighth Avenue, New York 10011
NINTH PRINTING

COLONEL CHABERT

"*L*ook! There's that old greatcoat again!" .This exclamation was made by a clerk belonging to the class called *gutter-jumpers* in French offices, who was at that moment heartily devouring a piece of bread. He pulled off a wad, rolled it into a ball, and fired it gleefully through the transom of the window he was leaning on. The pellet was well aimed, and bounced almost as high as the window after hitting the head of a stranger crossing the courtyard of a building in the Rue Vivienne, the address of Monsieur Derville, attorney-at-law.

"Simonnin, stop playing stupid tricks on people or you're out the door. No matter how poor a client is, he's still a man, damn it!" said the head clerk, pausing in his addition of a list of expenses.

The average gutter-jumper, like Simonnin, is a boy of thirteen or fourteen under the special tutelage of the head clerk, whose errands and love letters keep him busy carrying writs to the bailiffs and petitions to the Court. He has the habits of a Parisian street urchin and the inclinations of a con man. This child is almost always ruthless, headstrong, unmanageable, an inventor of bawdy rhymes, impudent, greedy, and lazy. Yet almost all the little clerks have an old mother lodging on the fifth floor somewhere, with whom they share their pittance of thirty or forty francs a month.

"If he's a *man*, why'd you call him *old greatcoat*?" asked Simonnin with the smirk of a schoolboy catching out his teacher. And he went on eating his bread and cheese, leaning his shoulder against the window frame— for he rested standing like a cab-horse—with one leg raised and leaning against the toe of his other shoe.

"What trick should we play on that fellow?" whispered Godeschal, the third clerk, pausing in the middle of an argument he was improvising for an appeal being drafted by a fourth clerk—copies of which were being made by two neophytes from the provinces. He went on improvising, ". . . *But in his noble and benevolent wisdom, His Majesty, Louis the Eighteenth* . . . write out all the letters—you, Desroches, the brains making the draft! . . . *when he assumed the reins of his realm, be it understood* . . . what did that old joker ever understand? . . . *the high mission to which he was called by Divine Providence!* . . . . . . a note of admiration and six periods. They are pious enough at the Court to let us put in six . . . *and his first thought, as is proved by the date of the ruling hereafter designated, was to repair the damages caused by the terrible and sorry disasters of our revolutionary times by restoring to his loyal and numerous adherents . . .* 'numerous' is flattering and should please the Court . . . *all their unsold property, whether in the public domain, in territory owned or acquired by the crown, or in the endowments of public institutions, for we are and we proclaim ourselves competent to declare that this is the spirit and meaning of the famous and truly loyal ruling rendered on . . .* Wait," said Godeschal to the three clerks, "that rascal of a sentence is over a page long. Okay," he went on, licking the back of the notebook so he could turn the thick page of stamped paper, "okay, if you want to play a good joke on him, tell him that the chief can only see his clients between two and three in the morning—we'll see if the old codger comes back." Godeschal went on with the sentence he had begun, "*rendered on . . .* Are you with me?" he asked.

"Yes," cried the three copiers. Everything was going on at once: the appeal, the gossip, and the conspiracy.

"*Rendered . . .* when? Papa Boucard, what's the date of the ruling? Let's dot our i's, by golly, it fills up pages!"

"*By golly!*" repeated one of the copiers before Boucard, the head clerk, could answer.

"What, you've written *by golly*?" cried Godeschal, looking at one of the novices with a stern and amused expression.

"Mmmm . . . yes," said Desroches, the fourth clerk, leaning over his neighbor's copy. "He has written: *We must dot our i's,* and *by colly* with a *c.*" All the clerks burst out laughing.

"How's that? Monsieur Huré, you think *by golly* is a legal term and you say you're from Mortagne!" cried Simonnin.

"Scratch it out properly!" said the head clerk. "If the judge responsible for processing this appeal sees things like that, he'll think we are mocking the whole profession. You'll get the chief in trouble. Come on, no more stupid mistakes, Monsieur Huré! No Norman takes writing an appeal so lightly. It is the law's first line of defense."

"*Rendered on . . . on?*" asked Godeschal. "Tell me when, Boucard."

"June 1814," answered the first clerk, without pausing in his work.

A knock at the office door interrupted this prolix appeal. Five hungry clerks with curly hair and bright, mocking eyes lifted their noses toward the door after crying together in a ringing voice, "Come in!" Boucard kept his face buried in a pile of papers—'odds and ends' in French legal jargon—and continued to address the expense account he was working on.

The office was a large room graced with the traditional stove that furnishes all these dens of chicanery. The stove pipes crossed the room diagonally and were connected to a bricked-up chimney, on whose mantle various bits of bread, triangles of Brie, fresh pork chops, glasses, bottles, and the head clerk's cup of chocolate could be seen. The odor of these food items blended so well with the stench of the overheated stove and the peculiar perfume of offices and old paper, that the stink of a fox would have gone unnoticed. The floor was already covered with mud and snow tramped in by the clerks. Near the window stood the head clerk's rolltop desk, and against its back was the little table belonging to the second clerk. At the moment, the second clerk was off at Court. It was between eight and nine in the morning.

The office was decorated exclusively with those large yellow posters announcing real estate foreclosures, sales, settlements held in trust, final or interim judgments—the glory of a lawyer's office! Behind the head clerk the entire wall was covered from top to bottom with shelves and pigeonholes. A seemingly infinite number of tickets hung from each crammed compartment, some with the red, taped ends that give legal dossiers a special appearance. The lower shelves were full of yellowed cardboard boxes rimmed with blue paper and labeled with the names of important clients whose juicy cases were stewing at that very moment. The dirty windowpanes admitted little light. In February there are very few offices in Paris where one can write without the help of a lamp before ten o'clock in the morning, for they are all uniformly neglected. Everyone goes to lawyer's offices, but no one stays; no one takes a personal interest in their day-to-day upkeep. Neither the lawyer, the counsel for the defense, nor the clerks pay much attention to the appearance of a place that is classroom for the young, waiting room for the clients, and laboratory for the Master himself. The crude furnishings are handed down so scrupulously from one generation of lawyers to the next that some offices still have boxes of remainders, machines for twisting parchment, and bags left by the plaintiffs at the Châtelet (abbreviated *Chlet*), as the First Court of Appeal under the old order was known.

There was something about this dingy office—so typically thick with dust—that was repulsive to the clients, making it one of the most hideous Parisian monstrosities. Indeed, if there were no damp sacristies where prayers are measured out and sold like spices, no secondhand shops with their display of rags that mock our illusions of life's festivity, if these sinkholes of the poetic did not exist, a lawyer's office would be the most terrible of all social bazaars. But the same might be said of gambling dens, the Courts, the lottery office, and the brothels. Why? Perhaps because in these places the drama being enacted in the soul of man gives him only a bit part; this would also explain the simplicity of great thinkers and men of great ambition.

"Where's my penknife?"

"I'm eating my breakfast!"

"Go to Hell! There's a smudge on the copy!"

"Shhh! Gentlemen."

These various exclamations were made simultaneously, just as the old client shut the door with the kind of humility that hobbles the movements of an unhappy man. The stranger tried to smile, but the muscles of his face fell as he looked in vain for some signs of propriety on the relentlessly callow faces of the six clerks. Accustomed, no doubt, to judging men, he addressed himself very politely to the gutter-jumper, hoping to get a civil answer from him.

"Sir, is your master in?"

The malicious gutter-jumper answered the poor man only by repeatedly tapping the fingers of his left hand on his ear, as if to say, "I'm deaf."

"What do you want, sir?" asked Godeschal, who posed this question while devouring a mouthful of bread big enough to load a blunderbuss, waving his knife about, and sticking one foot in the air almost as high as his eyes.

"I come here, sir, for the fifth time," answered the client. "I wish to speak to Monsieur Derville."

"On business?"

"Yes, but I can explain it to no one but Monsieur . . ."

"The chief is sleeping. If you wish to consult him on some difficulty, he does no serious work until midnight. But if you want to tell us about your case, we might help you as easily as he."

The stranger remained impassive. He looked timidly around him, like a dog who has slipped into a strange kitchen and fears being kicked. Thanks to their station, lawyer's clerks are never afraid of thieves. They did not suspect the man in the greatcoat and left him to examine the place. He was clearly tired, and was vainly scanning the room for a chair to sit on. Attorneys make a point of leaving very few chairs in their offices. The common client, kept waiting on his feet, goes away grumbling. Of course then he does not waste anybody's time, which, as an old lawyer put it, is not deducted from the fee.

"Monsieur," he answered, "I have already had the honor of advising you that I can only explain my business to Monsieur Derville. I will wait until he is up."

Boucard had finished his addition. He smelled his chocolate, left his caneback chair, came to the chimney, sized up the old man, looked at the greatcoat, and made an indescribable grimace. He probably thought that no matter how you squeezed this client, you couldn't wring a sou out of him. He then interjected a few words intended to rid the office of a bad customer.

"They are telling you the truth, sir. The chief works

only during the night. If your business is serious, I advise you to return at one o'clock in the morning."

The plaintiff looked at the head clerk with a bewildered expression, and stood motionless for a moment. The clerks, used to all the changes in physiognomy and singular whims produced by indecision or daydreaming, continued to eat, making as much noise with their jaws as horses in a stall, and no longer bothered about the old man.

"Sir, I will come back this evening," the old man said at last, with the tenacious desire peculiar to unhappy people to find humanity at fault. The poor have only one stab at irony—forcing Justice and Benevolence into patent falsehoods. Once the wretches have convicted society of perjury, they throw themselves more readily on the mercy of God.

"What a dimwit," said Simonnin, without waiting for the old man to shut the door.

"He looks like death warmed over," said the last clerk.

"He's some colonel who wants his back pay," said the head clerk.

"No, he's a retired concierge," said Godeschal.

"I'll bet you he's a nobleman!" cried Boucard.

"I bet he was a porter," replied Godeschal. "Only porters are endowed by nature with shabby greatcoats as greasy and frayed on the bottom as that old fellow's!

And did you see his leaky boots, and that cravat he wears as a shirt? He's surely been sleeping under bridges."

"He could have been a nobleman and still knocked on our door. It's been known to happen."

"No," went on Boucard in the midst of laughter, "I maintain that he was a brewer in 1789, and a colonel under the Republic."

"I'll bet tickets to a show all around that he was not a soldier," said Godeschal.

"Done!" Boucard replied.

"Monsieur! Monsieur!" cried the little clerk out the open window.

"What are you doing, Simonnin?" asked Boucard.

"I'm calling him back to ask him if he's a colonel or a porter—he must know."

All the clerks dissolved in laughter. As for the old man, he was already climbing back up the stairs.

"What'll we say to him?" cried Godeschal.

"Leave it to me!" answered Boucard.

The poor man came in timidly, his eyes lowered, perhaps not to betray his hunger by looking too greedily at the food.

"Monsieur," Boucard said to him, "would you be good enough to give us your name, so that our Master may know . . ."

"Chabert."

"Isn't that the colonel who died at Eylau?" asked Huré, who had said nothing so far and was eager to get in on the joking.

"The same, Monsieur," answered the good man with old-fashioned simplicity. And he withdrew.

"Whew!"

"Beaten!"

"Poof!"

"Oh!"

"Ah!"

"Bam!"

"The old rascal!"

"Ting-a-ling, ling!"

"Done in!"

"Monsieur Desroches, you'll go to the show without paying," said Huré to the fourth clerk, giving him a slap on the shoulder that would have killed a rhinoceros.

There was a storm of cries, laughter, and exclamations that would take all the onomatopoeia of the language to describe.

"What show are we going to?"

"To the Opera!" cried the head clerk.

"In the first place," replied Godeschal, "I haven't said which show. If you like, I could take you to see Madame Saqui."

"Madame Saqui isn't a show," said Desroches.

"What is a show?" replied Godeschal. "Let's first

settle this *point of order.* What did I bet, gentlemen? A show. And what is a show? Something you see . . ."

"But by that logic, you could simply take us to see the water running under Pont-Neuf," Simonnin broke in.

"Something seen for money," Godeschal added.

"But you can see many things for money that are not a show. The definition is not precise," said Desroches.

"Just listen to me!"

"You're talking nonsense, my boy," said Boucard.

"Is Curtius' a show?" asked Godeschal.

"No," replied the head clerk, "It's a bunch of statues."

"I bet you a hundred francs," Godeschal went on, "that Curtius' Waxworks belongs to the group of things that fall under the rubric of 'show' or 'theater.' It is something you pay different prices to see . . ."

"Blah, blah, blah," said Simonnin.

"Be careful I don't smack you!" said Godeschal.

The clerks shrugged their shoulders.

"Besides, it's not clear that the old monkey isn't playing a joke on us," he said, dropping his argument, which was drowned out by laughter anyhow. "Listen, Colonel Chabert is dead and his wife is remarried to Count Ferraud, Councillor of State. Madame Ferraud is one of the firm's clients!"

"The case is remanded until tomorrow," said Boucard. "To work, gentlemen! Confound it, we get nothing done around here! Let's finish this appeal; it's supposed to be handed in before the sitting of the Fourth Chamber, and the judgment is being pronounced today. Come on, let's get going!"

"And if he really were Colonel Chabert, wouldn't he have given that joker Simonnin a good kick in the behind when he played deaf?" said Desroches, considering this remark more conclusive than Godeschal's.

"Since nothing is settled," Boucard went on, "let's agree to go to the upper boxes of the Comédie-Française to see Talma in *Nero*. Simonnin will sit in the pit." And with that the head clerk sat down at his desk, and the others followed suit.

"*Rendered in June, One Thousand Eight Hundred and Fourteen* . . . all in letters," said Godeschal. "Are you with me?"

"Yes," answered the two copy clerks and the engrosser, whose pens once again began to scratch the stamped paper, filling the office with a noise like a hundred beetles caught by schoolboys in paper cones.

"*And we hope*," Godeschal went on after reading it over, "*that the Gentlemen of the Court will not be less magnanimous than the august author of the decree, and that they will bring justice against the wretched pretensions of the Chancellery of the Legion of Honor by interpreting the law in the wider sense that we set forth herein* . . ."

"Monsieur Godeschal, would you like a glass of water?" said the little clerk.

"That joker, Simonnin!" said Boucard. "Here, get your thick-soled hooves in action, take this packet, and waltz on over to Les Invalides."

". . . *that we set forth herein*," Godeschal continued. "Add: *submitted on behalf of Madame la Vicomtesse . . . in full . . . de Grandlieu . . .*"

"What!" cried the head clerk, "you're thinking of making an appeal in the case of the Vicomtesse de Grandlieu against the Legion of Honor—that case could make or break the office! You're a fool! Be good enough to save your copies and your notes. Keep them for the case of Navarreins against Les Hospices. It's late. I'll write up a little petition with a few *whereas* clauses, and be off to the Palais myself." This scene represents one of a thousand delightful moments that prompt us later, when we look back on our youth, to say, "Those were the good old days!"

$\mathcal{A}$t around one o'clock in the morning, the self-styled Colonel Chabert knocked at the door of Monsieur Derville, attorney to the Court of Appeals in the Department of the Seine. The porter answered that Monsieur Derville had not yet returned. The old fellow claimed he had an appointment and was shown upstairs to the office of that famous lawyer who, despite his youth, was reputed to be one of the most powerful minds on the Court.

After ringing, the distrustful applicant was more than a little surprised to see the head clerk busy arranging on the dining-room table his master's numerous dossiers on cases coming up the following day. The clerk, no less surprised, greeted the Colonel and asked him to take a seat, which he did.

"My word, Monsieur, I thought you were joking yesterday, advising me to come now for a consultation," said the Colonel with the false good humor of a ruined man forcing himself to smile.

"The clerks were joking and telling the truth, too," replied the head clerk, continuing his work. "Monsieur

Derville chooses this time to examine his cases, study their merits, devise strategy, and decide on the line of defense. His prodigious intellect is freer at this time, when he has the peace and quiet needed for good ideas. Since he opened his practice, you're the third person who's been given a midnight consultation. After coming home, the chief will discuss each case, read everything, spend perhaps four or five hours over this business, then he'll ring for me and explain his intentions. In the morning, from ten until two, he listens to his clients, then he spends the rest of the day in meetings. He spends his evenings going into society to keep up contacts. So only the late night is left for reviewing his trials, leafing through the Legal Code, and laying his battle plans. He doesn't want to lose a single case; he has a real love of his art. He doesn't take on every case that comes along, as his colleagues do. That's his life: exceptionally active. He earns a great deal of money."

Hearing this explanation, the old man remained silent, and his strange face assumed an expression so bereft of intelligence that the clerk, after a brief inspection, took no more notice of him.

A few minutes later, Derville came home in evening dress. His head clerk opened the door for him and hurried to finish arranging the files. The young attorney was dumbfounded for a moment to see this singular client waiting for him in the dim light. Colonel Chabert sat perfectly still, like one of the wax figures Godeschal had wanted to show his fellow clerks. This stillness would not have been so astonishing had it not completed the otherworldly impression made by the man's whole person. The old soldier was dry and lean. His forehead, deliberately hidden under the hair of his smooth wig, gave him a mysterious look. His eyes seemed covered with a transparent film or dirty enamel, whose bluish cast gleamed in the candlelight. The pale face, ghostly and knifelike—if I may use such an odd expression—seemed almost dead. His neck was tightly wound with a shabby black silk cravat. Beneath this rag his body was so well hidden in darkness that a man of imagination would have thought the head itself was just a play of shadows, or maybe an unframed Rembrandt. The brim of his hat cast a black furrow on his brow. This strange effect, although natural, sharply contrasted with the white wrinkles, the cold lines, and colorless tone of his cadaverous physiognomy. And the absence of all movement in the body, of all warmth in the look, mingled with a certain expression of melancholy madness and the progressive symptoms of idiocy, made his face seem unutterably doomed. Yet an observer, especially an attorney, would have found signs of the poverty that had stricken this face, the way marble is eventually eroded by falling raindrops. A doctor, an author, a judge would have read a whole drama in that aspect of sublime horror—like those fantastic creatures painters enjoy scribbling while chatting with their friends.

Seeing the attorney, the stranger shuddered with a movement of the sort that poets make when an unexpected noise rouses them from a fruitful, silent, midnight reverie. The old man promptly stood up to greet the young man. But since the leather lining the inside of his hat was probably quite greasy, his wig stayed glued to it and revealed his horribly mutilated skull. It was marked by a diagonal scar running from the nape of the neck to just over the right eye, forming a prominent and inflamed seam across his head. The sudden removal of this dirty wig, which the poor man wore to hide his ghastly wound, gave the two gentlemen of the law no inclination to laugh. The first thought that came to mind was, "That's how he must have lost his wits!"

"If he isn't Colonel Chabert, he must be some other brave trooper!" thought Boucard.

"Monsieur," Derville said to him, "to whom have I the honor of speaking?"

"To Colonel Chabert."

"Who?"

"The one who died at Eylau," answered the old man.

Hearing this singular phrase, the clerk and the attorney exchanged glances, as if to say, "He's mad!"

"Monsieur," the Colonel continued, "I would like to confide the secret of my situation only to you."

One thing worth noting is the natural intrepidness of lawyers. Whether from the habit of meeting a great many people, the profound feeling of protection granted them by the law, or from confidence in their ministry, they go everywhere without fear, like priests and physicians. Derville made a sign to Boucard, who left them alone.

"Monsieur," the attorney went on, "during the day I am not so jealous of my time, but in the middle of the night I feel each minute is precious. So be brief and concise. Give me the facts without any digression. I will ask you myself for any clarifications I consider necessary. Speak." After offering his singular client a seat, the young man sat down at the table himself; but while attending to the deceased Colonel's words, he leafed through his files.

"Monsieur," said the dead man, "perhaps you know that I commanded a regiment at Eylau. I was instrumental in the success of Murat's famous charge which turned the battle in our favor. Unfortunately for me, my death is a matter of historical record, reported in detail in *Victoires et Conquêtes*. We broke through the three Russian lines, which immediately re-formed, forcing us back in the opposite direction. Just as we were coming toward the Emperor, having scattered the Russians, I encountered the main body of the enemy's cavalry. I rushed at those obstinate men. Two Russian officers, real giants, attacked me. One of them swung his saber at my head and cut my skull deeply, even slicing through the black silk cap I was wearing. I fell from my horse. Murat came to my aid—by riding over my body, he and all his followers, 1500 men, maybe more! My death was announced to the Emperor, who as a precaution (he was awfully fond of me, the chief!) wanted to know if there were some chance of saving the man he had to thank for this vigorous attack. He sent two surgeons to find me and bring me to the field hospital, saying to them, perhaps too casually, 'Go and see whether by any chance my poor Chabert is still alive.' Those damned medics, who had just seen me trampled beneath the horses' hooves of two regiments, no doubt dispensed with checking my pulse and declared that I was quite dead. My death certificate was then probably made out in accordance with the rules of military jurisprudence."

Hearing his client express himself with perfect lucidity and relate such strange yet apparently credible facts, the young attorney put down his files, leaned his left elbow on the table, cupped his chin in his hand, and looked steadily at the Colonel.

"Do you know, Monsieur," he said to him, interrupting his story, "that I am the lawyer of Countess Ferraud, Colonel Chabert's widow?"

"My wife! Yes, Monsieur. And after a hundred fruitless attempts with other lawyers who thought I was mad, I decided to come to you. I will speak to you of my misfortunes later; first let me establish the facts and explain to you not how they seem to have happened, but how they actually did. Certain circumstances, known only to the heavenly Father, I suppose, oblige me to present several hypotheses. Well, Monsieur, the wounds I received probably gave me tetanus, or induced something like, I think it's called catalepsy. Otherwise, how is it conceivable that I should have been stripped of my clothing and thrown into a common grave?

"Here allow me to interject a detail that I could have known only after the event which might as well be called my death. In Stuttgart, in 1814, I met a former quartermaster from my regiment. This dear man, the only one who would recognize me—I'll say more about him soon—explained to me the extraordinary way I was saved. Apparently my horse had been shot in the flank the moment I was wounded myself. Horse and rider were thus knocked over like a house of cards. Wherever I fell, whether to the left or the right, I must have been covered by my horse's body, which prevented me from being crushed by galloping cavalry or hit by stray bullets. When I woke up, Monsieur, I was in a position and a setting which I couldn't convey to you if I talked till dawn. The little air I was breathing was foul. I wanted

21

to move but had no room. Opening my eyes, I saw nothing. The lack of air was the most dangerous thing, and the most pressing indication of my position. I could get no fresh air, and figured I was going to die. This thought wiped out the unbearable pain that had awakened me. My ears were buzzing horribly. I heard, or thought I heard—though I can't swear to it—groans coming from the pile of corpses I was lying in. Even though the memory of these moments is murky, and despite the fact I must have endured even greater suffering, there are nights when I still think I hear those muffled moans! But there was something more awful: a silence that I have never experienced anywhere else, the perfect silence of the grave. At last able to lift my hand, I felt dead flesh, and then a gap between my head and the corpses above. I explored this empty space I'd been miraculously left. It seems that thanks to the careless haste of our burial, two dead men above me were propped against each other like the base of a house of cards. Scrabbling around me at once, for there was no time to lose, I felt a huge, detached arm. I owe my rescue to that bone. Without it I would have perished! But with a fury I'm sure you can imagine, I plowed my way through the corpses separating me from the surface. A layer of earth had no doubt been thrown over us—I say 'us' as if the others were still alive! I still do not know how I could have dug through all that flesh. It formed a barrier between me and life.

But I went at it, Monsieur, and here I am. It was as though I had three arms! I used my lever adroitly, finding a little air between the corpses I pushed aside, and I breathed only sparingly. When I saw daylight at last, it was through the snow, Monsieur!

"At this moment I realized that my head was gashed open. Luckily, my blood, the blood of my comrades, or perhaps some skin torn off my horse—who knows?—had coagulated and acted as a natural plaster. In spite of this protection, I fainted when my skull came in contact with the snow. The little warmth I had left eventually melted the snow around me, and when I regained consciousness I found myself in the middle of a small hole. I lay there and kept shouting as long as I could. But it was only dawn and I had little chance of being heard. Wasn't there anyone in the fields? I pushed myself up with my feet standing on the solid backs of dead men. This was no time to respect the dead. Monsieur, I can't describe my sorrow, my fury, watching those damned Germans running away time and again, oh yes, time and again, because they heard my voice but saw no one. Finally I was freed by a woman brave enough or curious enough to approach my head, which seemed to have pushed up out of the earth like a mushroom. This woman went to fetch her husband, and together they carried me into their poor hovel. It seems I had a relapse of catalepsy—allow me to use this expression to depict for you a state that is completely unfamiliar to me but which seems to be the illness my hosts have described. For six months I hovered between life and death, not speaking, or incoherent when I did speak. At long last my hosts got me admitted to the hospital at Heilsberg.

"You understand, Monsieur, that I had risen from the bowels of this pit as naked as the day I was born. It took six months for me to recover my wits enough to remember I was Colonel Chabert. And one fine morning when I tried to get my nurse to show me more respect than she usually granted us poor devils, Monsieur, all my companions began to laugh.

"Luckily for me, my surgeon was interested in his patient, and out of pride in his work, guaranteed my recovery. When I told him about my previous life, this fine man, named Sparchmann, verified in the legal forms required by the law of his country the miraculous way I had escaped from the common grave, the day and hour I had been found by my benefactress and her husband, the nature and exact position of my wounds, and added to these depositions a description of my person.

"Of course I have none of these important papers, nor the declaration I made at a notary's office in Heilsberg to establish my identity. From the day I was run out of that town by the war, I have wandered like a vagabond, begging for my bread. I was treated as a madman when I told my tale, and couldn't earn a sou to obtain the papers that could prove my claims and restore me to life in society. My sufferings often stranded me for six months at a time in small towns, where care was lavished on French invalids, but where they laughed in my face when I claimed to be Colonel Chabert. For a long time that laughter, those doubts, would put me in such a rage that it did me serious harm. I was even locked up in Stuttgart as a madman. I'm sure you can judge from my story that there were ample reasons for locking such a man up!

"After two years in prison hearing my keepers call out a thousand times, 'There's a poor man who thinks he's Colonel Chabert!' to people who would answer, 'Oh, the poor soul!' I was convinced of the impossibility of my own story. I became melancholy, resigned, and somewhat at peace. I even gave up calling myself Colonel Chabert in order to get out of prison. Oh, Monsieur, to see Paris again was a dream I . . ." Leaving this sentence unfinished, Colonel Chabert fell into a deep reverie, which Derville silently respected.

"One fine day, Monsieur," the client continued, "one spring day, they gave me ten thalers and showed me the door, pleased that I was talking quite reasonably on all sorts of subjects and no longer calling myself Colonel Chabert. Let me tell you, my name can still be disagreeable to me. I wanted not to be myself. Knowing what I had lost was simply killing me. I would have been happy if my illness had deprived me of any memory of my past life! I would have gone into the army under an assumed name, and who knows? Perhaps I would have become a Field Marshal in Austria or Russia."

"Monsieur," said the attorney, "you are confusing me. I feel like I've been dreaming. Just hold on a moment."

"You are the only person," said the Colonel with a sorrowful look, "who has had the patience to listen to me. I haven't found a lawyer willing to advance me ten napoleons to send to Germany for the necessary documents to begin my lawsuit . . ."

"What lawsuit?" said the attorney, who had forgotten his client's present painful position while listening to his past sufferings.

"Monsieur, the Countess Ferraud is my wife! She possesses 30,000 pounds a year that belong to me, and she won't give me a sou. When I tell these things to lawyers, to men of good sense; when I propose that I, a beggar, should sue a count and countess; when I, a dead man, rise up against a death certificate, marriage licenses, and birth certificates, they show me the door—either with that cold politeness used to get rid of some unfortunate, or brutally, if they feel they're dealing with a felon or a fool, depending on their character. I've been buried beneath the dead, but now I'm buried beneath the living; beneath certificates, facts—

the whole society would rather have me buried underground!"

"Monsieur, please go on now," said the lawyer.

"*Please*," cried the unhappy old man, taking Derville's hand, "this is the first polite word I've heard since . . ."

The Colonel wept. His voice choked with gratitude. That penetrating and inarticulate eloquence of glance, of gesture, even of silence, finally convinced Derville, and touched him deeply.

"Listen to me, Monsieur," he said to his client, "this evening I won 300 francs at cards; I may certainly use half of that to make a man happy. I shall begin the inquiries and proceedings necessary to procure the papers you speak of, and until they arrive I will give you a hundred sous a day. If you are Colonel Chabert, you will know how to forgive the modesty of such a loan from a young man who has yet to make his fortune. Go on with your story."

The self-styled Colonel sat still a moment, dumbfounded: the extremity of his misfortunes had stripped him of his faith in mankind. If he was still pursuing his military reputation and his fortune, the effort probably only sprang from that inexplicable feeling buried in all men's hearts pushing them on toward greatness; that instinctive passion for glory to which we owe the discoveries of astronomy, alchemy, and physics. In his mind, ego was nothing but a secondary object, just as the vanity of success and the pleasure of winning become more valuable to the gambler than the stakes he has wagered. The young lawyer's words were like a miracle to this man rebuffed for ten years by his wife, by the law, by the whole social world. Imagine the young lawyer offering those ten pieces of gold he had been refused for so long by so many people in so many ways! The Colonel was like some lady who, having suffered from fever for fifteen years, believes she has simply exchanged one illness for another the day she is cured. There are felicities that arrive even when one no longer believes in them; they come like a thunderclap and are all-consuming. The poor man's gratitude was too great for him to express. To a superficial observer he may have seemed cold, but Derville saw this stupor as a sign of great integrity. A rogue would have found his voice.

"Where was I?" said the Colonel, with the naïveté of a child or a soldier—for there is often something of the child in a true soldier, and almost always something of the soldier in a child, especially in France.

"In Stuttgart. You were coming out of prison," answered the attorney.

"Do you know my wife?" asked the Colonel.

"Yes," Derville replied, nodding his head.

"How do you find her?"

"As charming as ever."

The old man made a gesture with his hand and

seemed to swallow some secret anguish with that solemn resignation typical of men tried in the blood and fire of battlefields.

"Monsieur . . ." he said with a certain cheerfulness, for after all, the poor Colonel was breathing once more; he had risen from the grave a second time; he had just melted a layer of snow even icier than the one that had frozen over his head; and he inhaled the air as if he were coming out of a dungeon. "Monsieur," he said, "if I had been a handsome fellow, I'd have had none of these misfortunes. Women believe in men when they sprinkle their speech with the word *love*. Then they scamper, they run, they rush off in all directions, they intrigue, they'll swear to anything, they play the very devil for a man who pleases them. How could I have interested a woman? My face had become a funeral dirge. I was dressed like a peasant; I looked more like an Eskimo than a Frenchman—I, who had passed for one of the prettiest fops of 1799! I, Chabert, Count of the Empire!

"Well, that very day when I was turned out on the streets like a dog, I met the quartermaster I have already mentioned. This comrade was called Boutin. The poor devil and I made the finest pair of broken-down hacks you've ever seen. I met him out walking; and although I recognized him, he couldn't make out who I was. We went to a tavern together. There, when I told him my name, Boutin's mouth split open in a burst of laughter like a mortar exploding. His amusement hurt me deeply,

Monsieur. It made me realize how much I had changed. I was unrecognizable even to the humblest and most grateful of my friends!

"I had once saved Boutin's life, but was only returning the favor. I will not tell you the whole story of how he did me this service. I was not a colonel at the time, but a simple cavalryman, like Boutin. He saved me from being stabbed in a not very respectable house in Ravenna. There were certain details of this adventure that were known only to the two of us, and when I brought them up, his disbelief vanished. Then I told him the accidents of my strange existence. Although my eyes and my voice were, he told me, singularly altered, though I no longer had any hair or teeth or eyebrows and was as white as an albino, after I had successfully answered a thousand questions, he finally recognized his Colonel in the beggar.

"He related his adventures, which were no less extraordinary than mine. He was on his way back from the frontiers of China, which he had tried to cross after escaping from Siberia. He told me of the disasters of the Russian campaign, and of Napoleon's first abdication. That news was one of the things that caused me the greatest anguish! We were two curious old wrecks who had rolled around the globe like stones storm-tossed through the ocean from one shore to the next. Between us we had seen Egypt, Syria, Spain, Russia, Holland, Germany, Italy, Dalmatia, England, China, Tartary,

Siberia; the only places we hadn't been were America and the Indies!

"At last, more nimble than I, Boutin took it upon himself to go to Paris as quickly as possible to inform my wife of my current state. I wrote Madame Chabert a very detailed letter—this was the fourth one, Monsieur! If I had had relatives, perhaps all this would not have happened. But I must confess to you that I was an orphan, a soldier whose patrimony was his courage, whose family was everyone, whose fatherland was France, and his only protector the good Lord. No, I am wrong, I did have a father: the Emperor! Ah, if only he were still here, the good man! And if he could see *his Chabert*, as he called me, in my present state, he would be furious! But what's the use? Our sun has set, we are all cold now. After all, you could even call my wife's silence political.

"Boutin set off. He was a very lucky fellow: he had two highly trained white bears to make him a living. I could not go with him; the pain I suffered did not allow me to walk far. I wept, Monsieur, when we parted, after walking along with him and his bears as far as I could. At Carlsruhe I had an attack of neuralgia and lay for six weeks on a straw pallet at an inn. I could go on forever, Monsieur, if I had to tell you all the miseries of my life as a beggar. Physical pain pales beside moral suffering, but arouses more pity since it can be seen. I remember weeping before a grand house in Strasbourg where I had once thrown a party—and was now given nothing, not even a piece of bread. What despair I endured! Having agreed with Boutin on the route I should follow, I went to every post office to ask if there were a letter and some money for me. I made my way to Paris without finding either. 'Boutin must be dead,' I said to myself. Indeed, the poor devil had succumbed at Waterloo. I learned of his death later, quite by chance. His mission to my wife was probably fruitless.

"At last I entered Paris, along with the Cossacks. For me, this was sorrow added to sorrow. Seeing the Russians in France, I entirely forgot I had no shoes on my feet or money in my pocket. Yes, Monsieur, my clothes were in tatters. The evening of my arrival I was forced to camp out in the woods at Claye. The cool night air probably caused another attack of some sort, which seized me just as I was crossing the Faubourg Saint-Martin. I fell almost senseless at the doorstep of an ironmonger's shop. When I came round, I was in a bed in the hospital. I stayed there rather contentedly for a month, but was soon thrown out. I had no money, but I was healthy and on the good streets of Paris, and so joyfully made my way to Rue du Mont-Blanc, where my wife should have been living in a house I owned. Bah! Rue du Mont-Blanc had become Rue de la Chaussée d'Antin. I could not find my house anywhere; it had been sold and demolished. Speculators had built houses in my gardens. Unaware that my wife was married to Monsieur Ferraud, I could obtain no information.

"At last I went to see an old lawyer who had been responsible for my affairs. The good soul had died after turning over his clientele to a younger man. He informed me, to my great surprise, of the court hearing on my estate, its settlement, my wife's marriage, and the birth of her two children. When I told him I was Colonel Chabert, he laughed so openly that I left without another word. My detention in Stuttgart made me think of Charenton Prison, and I resolved to act more cautiously. Then, Monsieur, knowing where my wife was living, I made my way to her house with a heart full of hope.

"Well," said the Colonel, with a gesture of concentrated rage, "when I called under an assumed name I was not received, and the day I used my own I was pushed out the door. I would spend whole nights glued to the corner of her gateway to watch the Countess coming home from the ball or the theater in the early morning. My gaze would plunge inside that carriage, which passed by with lightning speed, and barely catch a glimpse of the woman who is my wife and yet no longer mine. Oh, since that day I have lived for vengeance!" cried the old man in a strangled voice, suddenly standing before Derville. "She knows that I am alive; since my return she has received two letters written in my own hand. She does not love me anymore. As for me, I do not know if I love her or hate her! I desire her and curse her. She owes her fortune and her happiness to me, and she has not offered me the slightest help! Sometimes I don't know what will become of me!" At these words, the old soldier fell back in his chair and again sat motionless. Derville sat in silence, studying his client.

"This is a serious matter," he said at last, somewhat mechanically. "Even if the papers from Heilsberg are authentic, it is not clear to me that we will win the case right away. It will be heard by three different tribunals. I need to think about this case with a clear head; it is quite unusual."

"Well," the Colonel answered coldly, raising his head proudly, "if I lose, I may die, but not alone." Suddenly the old man disappeared, and the eyes of a young soldier ignited with the fires of desire and vengeance.

"We might have to compromise," said the lawyer.

"Compromise?" repeated Colonel Chabert. "Am I dead or am I alive?"

"Monsieur," continued the lawyer, "I hope you will follow my advice. Your cause is mine. You will soon perceive the interest I take in your situation, which is almost unparalleled in annals of the Courts. For the time being I will give you a message for my notary, who will remit to you on your receipt, fifty francs every ten days. It would not be proper for you to come here for assistance. If you are Colonel Chabert, you should be at no one's mercy. I will advance you these funds in the form of a loan. You have property to recover; you are a rich man."

This delicate gesture brought tears to the old man's

eyes. Derville rose abruptly, for it was not proper for a lawyer to show emotion. He went into his private office and returned with an unsealed letter, which he handed to Count Chabert. When the poor man held it in his hand, he felt through the paper two pieces of gold.

"Will you be good enough to describe the documents and give me the names of the town and the region?" said the lawyer.

The Colonel dictated the information and verified the spelling of the place-names. Then he took his hat in one thickly callused hand, looked at Derville, held out the other, and said simply, "Upon my faith, Monsieur, after the Emperor you are the man to whom I am most indebted! You are *a good soldier.*" The lawyer shook the Colonel's hand, led him to the landing, and held the light for him.

"Boucard," said Derville to his head clerk, "I've just heard a story that may cost me twenty-five louis. If I've been robbed, I won't miss the money, for I will have seen the most accomplished actor of our time."

When the Colonel was outside, under a streetlamp, he took the lawyer's two twenty-franc pieces out of the letter and looked at them a moment under the light. It was the first gold he had seen in nine years.

"Now I'll be able to smoke cigars!" he said to himself.

round three months after Colonel Chabert's midnight consultation with Derville, the notary charged with advancing the money the lawyer was paying his peculiar client came to see him to confer about a serious matter, and began by asking him to refund the 600 francs he had given the old soldier.

"Do you enjoy supporting the old army?" said the notary, laughing. His name was Crottat and he was a young man who had just bought the office where he had been head clerk—his boss having fled a dreadful bankruptcy.

"Thank you for reminding me of this business," answered Derville. "My philanthropy will not go beyond twenty-five louis. I fear I have already been duped by my patriotism." Just as Derville finished his sentence, he noticed the packets his head clerk had put on his desk. His eyes were struck by the stamps—oblong, square, triangular, red, blue—affixed to a letter by the Prussian, Austrian, Bavarian, and French post offices.

"Ah," he said, laughing, "here is the drama's denouement. Let's see if I've been tricked." He opened the letter, but couldn't read it as it was written in German. "Boucard, go and have this letter translated, and return promptly," he said, opening the door to his office and handing the letter to his head clerk.

The notary in Berlin to whom the lawyer had written informed him that the documents he had requested would arrive a few days after this notification. The papers, he said, were perfectly in order and cast in the requisite legal form to be admissible in a court of law. He also advised him that nearly all the witnesses to the facts set forth in these records were living in Eylau, Prussia, and that the woman to whom the Count Chabert owed his life was still living in one of the districts of Heilsberg.

"It looks like we're in business," exclaimed Derville, when Boucard had finished giving him the gist of the letter. "But tell me, my boy," he continued, addressing the notary, "I am going to need some information from your office. Wasn't it at that old rogue Roguin's . . ."

"We say the unfortunate, the *unhappy* Roguin," Monsieur Alexandre Crottat interrupted, laughing.

"Wasn't it at that unfortunate fellow's—who just bilked his clients of 800,000 francs, reducing several families to desperation—that Chabert's estate was settled? It seems to me that I noticed this among our Ferraud papers."

"Yes," replied Crottat, "I was third clerk then. I

copied that settlement and studied it thoroughly. Rose Chapotel, wife and widow of Hyacinthe Chabert, Count of the Empire, Grand Officer of the Legion of Honor—they were married without a contract and so held all property in common. To the best of my recollection, the assets amounted to 600,000 francs. Before his marriage, Count Chabert had made a will in favor of the alms-houses of Paris, according to which he left them a quarter of whatever fortune he possessed at the time of his death, with the State inheriting the other quarter. The will was contested, sold, then divided up—the attorneys really went at it. At the time of the settlement, the monster who was then governing France decreed that the Colonel's widow should have the portion bequeathed to the treasury."

"So the personal fortune of Count Chabert amounted to only 300,000 francs?"

"So it was, old fellow!" replied Crottat. "You lawyers are sometimes fair-minded after all, though you're accused of the opposite, pleading equally for either side."

ount Chabert, whose address could be read at the bottom of the first receipt he had given the notary, lived in the Faubourg Saint-Marceau, Rue du Petit-Banquier, with an old quartermaster of the Imperial Guard, now a dairyman, named Vergniaud. Once there, Derville was forced to go on foot in search of his client, since his coachman refused to drive on an unpaved street too deeply rutted for cab wheels. Looking all around the end of the street near the boulevard, the lawyer at last found an entrance between two walls built of bones and earth. The gateposts were damaged by passing carts, despite two protective pieces of wood. These gateposts supported a wooden beam covered by a tile coping, on which these words were written in red: VERGNIAUD, DAIRYMAN. Eggs were pictured to the right of this name and to the left, a cow, all painted in white.

The gate was open and had no doubt stood that way all day. At the end of a rather large courtyard a house stood facing the gate—if "house" is the right word for one of those hovels built in the seedier suburbs of Paris.

They are like nothing else, not even the most wretched rural shacks, whose poverty they share without their poetry. Indeed, cottages in the midst of fields still have a grace bestowed upon them by the purity of the air, the green shimmer of the vegetation, a hill, a twisting path, vines, a live hedge, the moss of thatched roofs, and rustic implements. But in Paris the horror of poverty is magnified. Although recently built, this house seemed to be falling into ruin. None of its materials had been used as intended but had been scavenged from the demolitions taking place in Paris daily. On a shutter made from a shop sign, Derville read: *Fancy Goods*. The windows were all uneven and bizarrely placed. The ground floor, which seemed to be the living quarters, was raised on one side above the earth, while on the other the rooms were sunk into a hill. Between the gate and the house lay a pool full of dung overflowing with rainwater and slops. The wall on which this wretched dwelling was propped—which seemed to be more solid than the others—was festooned with hutches where rabbits were breeding their large families. To the right of the gate was the barn with a loft above for fodder; it was attached to the house through a dairy. To the left were a poultry yard, a stable, and a pigsty with a roof finished, like the one on the house, with inferior, whitewashed boards, overlapping, and poorly thatched with rushes.

The courtyard was strewn with the elements of the

large common meal Parisians hurry to prepare each day. Those huge, bulging, white iron vats for carrying milk, and the cream pots with their linen stoppers were tossed everywhere in front of the dairy. The rags used to wipe them off fluttered in the sun, hanging on strings attached to posts. One of those docile horses found only in dairies had taken a few steps in front of his cart and was standing before the closed door of the stable. A goat browsed on shoots of the slender, dusty vine festooning the cracked yellow wall of the house. A cat was crouching on the cream pots and licking them clean. The chickens, startled by Derville's approach, flew off squawking, and the guard dog began to bark.

"The man who won the battle of Eylau lives here!" Derville said to himself, taking in the whole degrading spectacle at a glance.

The house was guarded by three young urchins. One, who had climbed to the top of a cart loaded with hay, was throwing stones into the chimney of the neighboring house, hoping they would fall into the cooking pot. The other was trying to lead a pig onto a cart which was resting on the ground, while the third, hanging onto the other end, was waiting for the pig to get in and tip the cart up. When Derville asked them if Monsieur Chabert lived there, none of them replied, and all three looked at him with a sort of intelligent stupidity—if I may pronounce these words in the same breath. Derville repeated his questions without success. Provoked by the sly air of the three scamps, he insulted them with the sort of remarks young men think they have the right to address to children, and the urchins broke their silence with a brutal laugh. Derville got angry.

The Colonel, hearing him, emerged from a small, low-ceilinged room near the dairy, and appeared on his threshold with indescribable military calm. He was holding in his mouth one of those highly seasoned, yet humble, white clay pipes called *jaw-burners* in smoker's parlance. He raised the visor of a horribly filthy cap, recognized Derville, and crossed the dungheap to join his benefactor, calling to the urchins in an affable voice, "Silence in the ranks!" The children instantly fell into a respectful silence, demonstrating the old soldier's power over them.

"Why haven't you written to me?" he said to Derville. "Go along by the cowhouse! The path is paved there," he exclaimed, noticing the indecision of the lawyer, who did not want to slop through the dungheap.

Jumping from place to place, Derville reached the Colonel's door. Chabert seemed uncomfortable receiving him in his own room. In fact, Derville noticed that it contained only a single chair. The Colonel's bed consisted of a pile of straw which his hostess had covered with two or three old carpets from God knows where—perhaps the kind used to cover the benches of their dairy carts. The floor was simply stamped earth. The white-washed walls, greenish and cracked, were so damp that the wall the Colonel slept against was carpeted with a rush mat. The famous greatcoat was hanging on a nail. Two broken-down pairs of boots lay in a corner. No trace of linens in sight. On the worm-eaten table, the *Bulletin of the Grand Army* reprinted by Plancher lay open, and seemed to constitute the Colonel's only reading. His face was calm and serene in the midst of this squalor. The visit to Derville seemed to have changed the character of his features, and the lawyer found traces there of a happy thought, a ray of hope.

"Does the pipe smoke bother you?" he said, directing his lawyer to the dilapidated chair.

"Colonel, you must be miserably uncomfortable here." These words were torn from Derville by the distrust natural to lawyers, and by the deplorable experience they acquire early in life from the ghastly untold tragedies they witness. "Here," he said to himself, "is a man who has surely spent my money satisfying the trooper's three cardinal virtues: wine, women, and cards."

"It is true, Monsieur, we are not living in luxury here. This is a bivouac made tolerable by friendship, but . . ." here the soldier shot a penetrating glance at the man of the law, "but I have done no one wrong. I have never refused anyone, and I sleep peacefully."

The lawyer thought it would be indelicate to ask his client to account for the sums he had advanced, so he merely said, "Why haven't you come to Paris, then, where you might live as cheaply as you do here, but in better accommodations?"

"But these good people welcomed me and fed me *gratis* for a year!" answered the Colonel. "How could I leave them just when I have a little money? And the father of those three urchins is an old *Egyptian* . . ."

"An Egyptian?"

"We gave that name to the troopers like me who returned from the Egyptian expedition. Not only are those of us who returned brothers of a sort, but Vergniaud was in my regiment. We have shared water in the desert. And I haven't finished teaching his scamps to read."

"He might have given you better lodgings for your money."

"Bah," said the Colonel, "his children sleep as I do, on straw. He and his wife have no better bed; they are very poor. They have taken on a bigger business than they can manage. But if I recover my fortune . . . well, enough!"

"Colonel, tomorrow or the day after, I should receive your documents from Heilsberg. The woman who saved you is still alive!"

"Damn money! To think I haven't got any!" he exclaimed, flinging his pipe on the ground. Now, to a smoker a seasoned pipe is a precious thing, but the gesture was so natural, the feeling so noble, that all smokers and even the Customs Office would have pardoned this crime against tobacco. The angels might even have picked up the pieces.

"Colonel, your case is exceedingly complicated," Derville said to him, leaving the room to walk out in the sun along the side of the house.

"It seems perfectly simple to me," said the solder. "They thought I was dead, but here I am! Give me back my wife and my fortune; give me the rank of general to which I am entitled, for I went beyond colonel in the Imperial Guard on the eve of the battle of Eylau."

"Things do not happen this way in the legal world," continued Derville. "Listen to me. Certainly I believe that you are Count Chabert, but the task at hand is to prove it in court to people who have an interest in denying your existence. Your documents will be disputed. This dispute will raise ten or twelve preliminary questions. Each question will be contested all the way up to the Supreme Court, and will involve costly trials that will drag on and on, no matter what I do. Your adversaries will ask for an inquiry which we cannot refuse, and which may require a commission from a Prussian Court to gather evidence. But even assuming the best— that the law will immediately recognize you as Colonel Chabert—can we predict how the question of Countess

Ferraud's quite innocent bigamy will be settled? In your case, the point of law is outside the Code and may be decided by the judge's sense of conscience, just as the jury does in certain odd criminal trials. You had no children in your marriage, and Count Ferraud has two; the judges can declare the marriage annulled in which the ties are weakest, in favor of the marriage in which they are strongest—since it was contracted in good faith. Will you be in a moral position to insist, at your age and in your present circumstances, on claiming a woman who no longer loves you? You will have your wife and her husband against you, two powerful people who could influence the Court. So there are many elements that would prolong the trial. You will have time to grow into an embittered old age."

"And what about my fortune?"

"Do you really believe you have a large fortune?"

"Did I not have an income of 30,000 pounds?"

"My dear Colonel, in 1799, before your marriage, you made a will that bequeathed a quarter of your property to the almshouses."

"That is true."

"Well, when you were reported dead, it was necessary to take an inventory of your properties, hold a liquidation sale, and give the almshouses their share. Your wife had no scruples about cheating the poor. She no doubt refrained from including cash at hand and jewelry, or most of your silver in the inventory, and had the furnishings estimated at two-thirds their actual price. That way she could pay lower inheritance taxes. And because of the estate evaluators' estimates, the inventory was established at a value of only 600,000 francs. Your widow had the right to half of that. She sold everything and then bought it back; she made a killing, and the almshouses had their 75,000 francs. Then, as the rest went to the State and you had made no mention of your wife in your will, the Emperor returned to your widow by decree the portion which had reverted to the public domain. So what are you now worth? Only 300,000 francs, minus expenses."

"And you call that justice?" said the Colonel, in amazement.

"Of course . . ."

"A fine thing!"

"So it is, my poor Colonel. You see that what you thought was simple enough, certainly is not. Madame Ferraud is even entitled to keep the portion she was given by the Emperor."

"But she was not a widow, the decree nullified . . ."

"I agree. But every cause can get a hearing. Listen to me. In these circumstances, I think that a settlement would be the best solution for both of you. You will get back more than you are entitled to."

"But that would be selling my wife!"

"With 24,000 francs a year, you would be in a position to find a woman who will suit you better than your own wife, and who will make you happier. I am prepared to see Countess Ferraud today in order to sound her out; but I did not want to undertake such a visit without informing you."

"Let us go see her together."

"As you are?" said the lawyer. "No, Colonel, no. You would lose your case altogether."

"Can I win my case, then?"

"On all counts," Derville replied. "But, my dear Colonel Chabert, you are overlooking one thing. I am not rich; I haven't been paid. If the Court offers you an advance against your fortune, they will grant it only after having recognized you as Colonel Chabert, Grand Officer of the Legion of Honor."

"But I am a Grand Officer of the Legion; I had forgotten about it," he said naïvely.

"Well, until then," replied Derville, "you still have to plead your case, pay lawyers, draw up and discharge documents, keep the process servers busy, and live. The expenses of preliminary hearings will add up, roughly, to more than 12,000 or perhaps 15,000 francs. I haven't got that much; I am crushed by the enormous interest on the money I borrowed to buy my business. And you— could you pay for it?"

Large tears fell from the poor soldier's faded eyes

and rolled down his lined cheeks. These difficulties discouraged him. The social and judicial world weighed on his chest like a nightmare.

"I will go to the foot of the column at the Place Vendôme," he cried, "and I will shout 'I am Colonel Chabert, who routed the Russians at Eylau!' The bronze statue will recognize me!"

"And they will probably lock you up in Charenton."

At this terrible name, the veteran's exaltation collapsed.

"Would there be no better possibilities for me at the Ministry of War?"

"The Ministry!" said Derville. "Go there, certainly. But take a formal document with you declaring your death certificate null and void. They would like nothing better than to annihilate the men of the Empire."

The Colonel stood for a moment speechless, motionless, his eyes glazed over, plunged into profound despair. Military justice is forthright, swift, harsh, and almost always fair; this was the only form of justice Chabert knew. Seeing the labyrinth of difficulties he had to enter, and seeing how much money he needed to do it, the poor soldier suffered a mortal blow to that power peculiar to man called *will*. It seemed impossible to him to survive a lawsuit, and a thousand times simpler to continue as a poor man, a beggar; to enlist as a trooper if some regiment would have him.

His physical and moral sufferings had already damaged some of his vital organs. He was on the verge of one of those maladies medicine has no name for, which attacks the fragile nervous system, and might as well be called *dejection*. As serious as this invisible (but real) illness already was, it was still curable by a happy conclusion. But any new, unforeseen obstacle would be enough to utterly destroy his vigorous constitution, breaking its weakened springs and producing those hesitations, those aimless, unfinished acts physiologists observe in men ruined by grief.

Recognizing in his client the symptoms of extreme dejection, Derville said, "Take heart, the solution to this business can only be favorable to you. You must trust me entirely, and blindly accept the outcome I think is in your best interests."

"Do as you like," said Chabert.

"Colonel, you are surrendering like a man going to the gallows."

"Shall I not be left, all the same, without a position or a name? Is that bearable?"

"I don't view it that way," said the lawyer. "We shall pursue an out-of-court settlement to annul your death certificate and your marriage so you can get what's owed you. Through Count Ferraud's influence you will even be reinstated as a general in the army, and no doubt you will receive a pension."

"Well all right, go ahead," replied Chabert. "I am entirely in your hands."

"I will send you a power-of-attorney to sign, then," said Derville. "Good-bye, keep up your spirits! If you need money, you can count on me."

Chabert squeezed Derville's hand warmly and continued to stand leaning against the wall, too weak to follow him except with his eyes. Like all men who have a scant understanding of legal affairs, he was frightened by this unforeseen struggle. Several times during this meeting the figure of a man standing in the street came forward from behind one of the gateposts, watching for Derville's departure, and now accosted him on his way out. He was an old man dressed in a blue jacket and a pleated white tunic like a brewer's, and on his head he wore an otter-skin cap. His face was brown, hollowed, and lined, but ruddy from hard work and tanned from the open air.

"Begging your pardon, Monsieur," he said to Derville, catching him by the arm, "if I take the liberty of speaking to you, but I thought when I saw you that you were a friend of our General."

"Well, in what way is he your concern? And who are you?" replied the wary lawyer.

"I am Louis Vergniaud," he answered first. "And I would have two words with you."

"Is it you who has lodged Colonel Chabert this way?"

"Begging your pardon, excuse me, Monsieur, he has the best room. I would have given him mine if I had one. I would have slept in the stable. A man who has suffered like him, who teaches my scamps to read, a general, an Egyptian, the first lieutenant I served under . . . What do you think? He has the best room of all. I have shared all I have with him. Unfortunately, it isn't much: bread, milk, eggs; well, you have to take the good with the bad! And we've done it with open arms. But he's offended us."

"Him?"

"Frankly, sir, yes. He noticed that I'd taken on a larger business than I can manage. Well, it worried him, and so he starts grooming the horse! I tried to stop him, but he says 'Bah, I'm not going to lie around like a good-for-nothing. I learned to curry a nag before you were born.' I had borrowed some money to pay off my dairy from a man named Grados—do you know him, sir?"

"My good man, I do not have the time to listen to you. Just tell me how the Colonel offended you!"

"He offended us, sir, as truly as my name is Louis Vergniaud. My wife has been in tears over it. He knew from the neighbors that we didn't have a sou to pay our debt. Without a word the old veteran saved up everything you were giving him, watched for the bill to come, and paid it off. What a trick! And my wife and me, we knew he had no tobacco, the poor old fellow, and was doing without. Oh, now—yes, he has his cigars every morning. I would rather sell myself . . . No! It's embarrassing. So, I wanted to ask you, seeing as how he said you were a good man, to lend us a hundred crowns so we could get him some clothes and furnish his room. He thought he'd paid off our debts, didn't he? Well, now we feel indebted to the old man! He shouldn't have played such a dirty trick on us. And we're his friends, too. On my honor, as truly as my name is Louis Vergniaud, I would sooner enlist than not pay you back your money."

Derville looked at the dairyman, and took a few steps back in order to get a better view of the house, the courtyard, the dungheaps, the stable, the rabbits, the children.

"Honestly, I think one of the greatest virtues is not to own property," the lawyer said to himself. "Go on, you will have your hundred crowns, and more. But I will not be the one to give it to you; the Colonel will be rich enough to help you, and I do not want to deprive him of the pleasure."

"Will that be soon?"

"Yes, indeed."

"Ah, my God, how happy my wife will be!"

And the weathered face of the dairyman seemed to expand.

"Now," Derville said to himself, climbing into his

cab, "let's pay a visit to our adversary. I'll hold my cards close to the chest, try to guess hers, and win the game in one round. But how should I frighten her? She's a woman. What are women most afraid of? Well, women are frightened by only one thing . . ."

He began to examine the Countess' position, and fell into one of those meditations great politicians give themselves to while laying their plans and trying to guess their enemies' secrets. Are lawyers not, in a way, statesmen charged with private business? A brief glance at the situation of Count Ferraud and his wife is in order here if we are to comprehend the full extent of the lawyer's brilliance.

Count Ferraud was the son of a former Councillor in the Parliament of Paris who had emigrated during the time of the Terror, and who had sacrificed his fortune to save his skin. The Count returned during the Consulate and remained loyal to the interests of Louis XVIII, in whose circle his father had moved before the Revolution. He belonged, then, to that party of the Faubourg Saint-Germain which nobly resisted the seductions of Napoleon. The young Count's reputation as an able man—he was then called simply Monsieur Ferraud— made him the object of the Emperor's advances, for the Emperor considered his conquest of the aristocracy to be a military victory. The Count was promised the restoration of his title, the remainder of his unsold property, and a minister's portfolio or a position as senator at some time in the future. The Emperor, however, ran aground.

At the time of Colonel Chabert's death, Monsieur Ferraud was a young man of twenty-six, without a fortune, endowed with an attractive appearance and a number of successes, so the Faubourg Saint-Germain viewed him as one of its crowning glories. Countess Chabert, however, had extracted such a good part of her husband's estate, that after eighteen months of widowhood she possessed an income of around 40,000 pounds. Her marriage to the young Count was not greeted as big news by the coteries of the Faubourg Saint-Germain. Napoleon was pleased with the marriage, and returned to Madame Chabert the portion of the Colonel's property that had gone to the State; but Napoleon's hopes were again thwarted. Madame Ferraud did not cherish only the lover in the young man, she had also been seduced by the idea of entering that disdainful society which, despite its degradation, still dominated the imperial Court. In this marriage her vanity was satisfied as much as her passion. She was set on becoming a *proper lady*. When the Faubourg Saint-Germain understood that the young Count's marriage was not a defection, its salons were opened to his wife.

Then came the Restoration. Count Ferraud's political fortunes were not immediately realized. He understood the position in which Louis XVIII found himself, and was one of the initiates waiting for the *abyss of the Revolution to close;* for this royal phrase, so ridiculed by liberals, made sound political sense. Nonetheless, the ruling cited in the long lawyerly preamble at the beginning of this story had returned to him two forests and a piece of land which had considerably increased in value while sequestered. At present, although Count Ferraud was a Councillor of State, a Director-General, he regarded this as only the beginning of his political career.

Preoccupied with his consuming ambition, he hired as his secretary a bankrupt attorney named Delbecq, a terribly clever man admirably acquainted with the resources of chicanery, to whom he entrusted all his private affairs. Self-interest kept this shrewd operator faithful to the Count. He hoped to succeed through his patron's influence, and made the Count's fortune his primary concern. His conduct so effectively falsified his former life that he was regarded as a man who had been slandered. The Countess, with the tact and finesse most women share to some degree, understood Delbecq, watched him closely, and handled him well enough to augment her private fortune. She managed to persuade him that she ruled her husband, Monsieur Ferraud, and promised to use her influence to have him appointed president of a lower court in one of the most important towns of France if he would devote himself entirely to her interests. Property values rose and the stock market fluctuated wildly during the first three years of the Restoration, and Delbecq never missed an opportunity to increase the Countess' fortune. He tripled his protectress' capital—all the more easily as she stopped at nothing to make money as quickly as possible. She used the remuneration from the Count's various positions to pay for household expenses so as to reinvest her dividends, with Delbecq blindly lending himself to these calculations of greed. Such men worry only about secrets whose discovery might compromise their own interests. Indeed, he found this thirst for gold natural and reasonable since it afflicts most Parisian women. And since a great fortune was needed to support Count Ferraud's pretensions, the secretary sometimes thought he saw in the Countess' greed evidence of her devotion to the man she loved. The Countess had buried the secrets of her conduct deep in her heart. There lay the secrets of life and death for her; there lay the crux of this story.

At the beginning of the year 1818, the Restoration was established on seemingly unshakable foundations; its principles of government, understood by lofty minds, appeared destined to lead France into an era of new prosperity, and Parisian society changed its complexion. Countess Ferraud found that she had managed to make a marriage of love, fortune, and ambition. Still young and beautiful, Madame Ferraud played the role of a woman of fashion, and lived with courtly grace. Rich in her own right, rich through her husband—who was touted as one of the ablest men of the Royalist party, a friend of the King, almost certain to be made a minister—she belonged to the aristocracy and shared its splendor. In the midst of this triumph, though, she was attacked by a moral cancer. There are certain feelings women will intuit despite the care men take to hide them. When the King first returned, Count Ferraud began having some regrets about his marriage. Colonel Chabert's widow had no connections. He was alone and unsupported as he made his way in a career full of obstacles and enemies. Then, perhaps, once he could judge his wife coolly, he had recognized certain flaws in her education that made her unfit to aid him in his schemes.

A remark he made about the marriage of Talleyrand enlightened the Countess, and proved to her that if he were still unmarried, she would never have become Madame Ferraud. What woman could forgive such regret? Does it not contain the seed of all insults, all crimes, all repudiations? And how this remark must have wounded the Countess, living in fear, as she did, of seeing her first husband again! She knew he was still alive and she had turned him away. When she heard nothing more from him, she was happy to believe he had died at Waterloo with the Imperial Eagles, in Boutin's company. Nonetheless, she schemed to bind the Count to her by the most powerful ties, by a chain of gold, hoping to be so rich that her fortune would make her second marriage indissoluble, if by chance Count Chabert should reappear. He had reappeared, and she could not explain to herself why the struggle she was dreading had not already begun. Suffering and sickness had perhaps delivered her from this man. Perhaps he was half mad; and Charenton might still vindicate her. She did not want to confide in Delbecq or in the police, for fear of exposing her vulnerability and precipitating the disaster. There are many women in Paris who, like Countess Ferraud, live on the edge of a moral abyss, or with some unknown monster in their closet. They gloss over the evil that gnaws at them, and are still able to laugh and enjoy themselves.

"There is something quite odd about Count Ferraud's position," Derville said to himself, emerging from his long reverie as his cab pulled up at the Ferraud mansion in Rue de Varenne. "If he is so rich and such a favorite of the King, how is it that he is not yet a Peer of France? It may be true, as Madame de Grandlieu has told me, that it is part of the King's strategy to enhance the importance of the Peerage by not handing out places indiscriminately. After all, the son of a Councillor of Parliament is not a Crillon or a Rohan. Count Ferraud can only enter the upper chamber surreptitiously. But if his marriage were annulled, might not the King give him the place of one of those old senators who have only daughters? Here's a tall tale to frighten our Countess," he said to himself as he climbed the front steps.

Derville had unwittingly put his finger on the hidden wound, his hand on the cancer consuming Madame Ferraud. She received him in a pretty winter dining room, where she was lunching while playing with a monkey chained to an iron climbing post. The Countess was wrapped in an elegant peignoir; her loosely pinned curls escaped from a bonnet giving her saucy look. She was fresh and smiling. Silver, gold, and mother-of-pearl glittered on the table, and all around her exotic flowers were planted in magnificent porcelain pots.

Seeing Colonel Chabert's wife, rich with his spoils, living in the lap of luxury and at the height of society, while the poor Colonel lived with a miserable dairyman among beasts, the lawyer said to himself, "There is no way that this pretty wife will ever admit that a man in an old greatcoat, a greasy wig, and boots with holes in them is her husband, or even her lover." A mischievous and mordant smile expressed the kind of half-philosophical and half-satirical ideas that come naturally to a man positioned to see behind the lies that most Parisian families use to conceal their lives.

"Good morning, Monsieur Derville," she said, offering the monkey some coffee.

"Madame," he said a little sharply, for he was

shocked by her rather frivolous tone, "I have come to speak to you about a serious matter."

"I am *terribly sorry*, but the Count is not here . . ."

"I am delighted to hear it, Madame. It would be *terrible* indeed if he were to be present at our meeting. Anyway, I know from Delbecq that you prefer to manage your own affairs without troubling the Count."

"Then I shall send for Delbecq," she said.

"He would do you no good, skillful as he is," replied Derville. "Listen to me, Madame, a word will suffice to make you take this seriously. Colonel Chabert is alive."

"Do you think you can make me serious by babbling such nonsense?" she said with a burst of laughter. But the Countess was suddenly struck by the strange lucidity of Derville's questioning gaze, which seemed to read the depths of her soul.

"Madame," he replied, with a cold and penetrating gravity, "you are unaware of the dangers that threaten you. I will not speak to you of the unquestionable authenticity of the documents or the conclusiveness of the proofs that attest to Count Chabert's existence. I am not a man to take up a losing cause, as you know. If you resist our efforts to nullify the death certificate, you will lose; and this first matter settled in our favor will ensure that we win the others."

"Well then, what do you wish to speak to me about?"

"Neither the Colonel nor you. Nor will I speak to you about memories, as a clever attorney might do, armed with the curious facts of this case, knowing the advantage he might derive from the letters you received from your first husband before you remarried."

"That's not true!" she said with all the violence of a coquette. "I never received a letter from Count Chabert. And if someone claims to be the Colonel, he must be some swindler, some freed convict like Coignard, perhaps. It makes me shudder to think of it. Can the Colonel rise from the dead, Monsieur? Bonaparte sent an aide-de-camp to call on me at the time of his death, and to this day I draw the pension of 3,000 francs from the government. I have been perfectly in the right to turn away all the Chaberts who have appeared, and I will turn away all who come in the future."

"Fortunately, Madame, we are alone. We can lie to our hearts' content," Derville said coldly, finding it amusing to fuel the Countess' rage and perhaps induce her to commit some indiscretion. Staying calm while their adversaries or their clients get carried away is a maneuver familiar to attorneys.

"Well, then, it is just the two of us," he said to himself, at that very moment setting a trap to show her the weakness of her position. "Proof of the delivery of the first letter exists, Madame," he replied aloud. "It contained some securities . . ."

"Securities? It contained no securities."

"Then you did receive this first letter," replied Derville, smiling. "You fall into the first trap a lawyer lays for you, and you think you can fight against justice."

The Countess blushed, paled, hid her face in her hands. Then she shook off her shame and replied with the sang-froid natural to such women, "Since you are attorney to the so-called Chabert, do me the honor of . . ."

"Madame," said Derville interrupting her, "at the moment I am still your attorney as much as I am the Colonel's. Do you imagine that I would wish to lose a client as valuable as you? You are not listening to me."

"Speak, Monsieur," she said graciously.

"Your fortune came to you from Count Chabert, and you have turned him away. Your fortune is immense and you are willing to let him go begging. Madame, lawyers can be quite eloquent when the cause is eloquent in itself, and here circumstances converge that can easily turn public opinion against you."

"But Monsieur," said the Countess, irritated by the way Derville kept raking her over the coals, "even if I admit that your Monsieur Chabert exists, the courts will uphold my second marriage because of the children, and I shall be let off with restoring 225,000 francs to Monsieur Chabert."

"Madame, we do not know how the courts will view the question. On one side we have a mother and her children, and on the other we have a man crushed by misfortunes, aged before his time by you and your rejections. Where will he find a wife? And can the judges go against the law? Your marriage to the Colonel has priority in the eyes of the law. And if you are seen to be at fault, you will have an unexpected adversary. Madame, I would like to shield you from this danger."

"A new adversary!" she exclaimed. "Who?"

"Count Ferraud, Madame."

"Monsieur Ferraud has too much affection for me and too much respect for the mother of his children . . ."

"Don't talk such nonsense," Derville said, interrupting her as lawyers do who are familiar with the depths of the human heart. "At the moment Monsieur Ferraud hasn't the slightest wish to break up your marriage and I am convinced that he adores you. But if someone came to him and said that his marriage can be annulled, that his wife will be reviled as a criminal in the court of public opinion . . ."

"He would defend me, Monsieur!"

"No, Madame."

"What reason could he have to desert me, Monsieur?"

"Why, to marry the only daughter of a Peer of

France, whose title would be transferred to him by order of the King."

The Countess blanched.

"Bull's-eye," Derville said to himself. "I've got you; the poor Colonel's case is won."

"Furthermore, Madame," he continued aloud, "he would have much less remorse since a man so covered with military glory—a General, a Count, a Grand Officer of the Legion of Honor—is not so bad as a last resort. And if this man demands his wife back . . ."

"Enough! Enough, Monsieur!" she said. "I will never have anyone but you as my lawyer. What can we do?"

"Compromise!" Derville replied.

"Does he still love me?" she asked.

"Well, I do not see how he can do otherwise."

At this remark the Countess raised her head. A ray of hope shone in her eyes. Perhaps she was counting on her feminine wiles and the tenderness of her first husband to help her win her case.

"I will await your orders, Madame. Let me know whether I should notify you of our proceedings or whether you will agree to come to my office to negotiate a settlement," Derville said, taking his leave of the Countess.

$\mathcal{E}$ight days after Derville's two visits, and on a fine morning in the month of June, the spouses, separated by almost supernatural accident, started out from opposite ends of Paris to meet in the office of their common attorney. The advance Derville had paid to Colonel Chabert allowed him to dress in keeping with his rank. The deceased arrived, then, driven in a very decent cab. His head was covered by a suitable wig. He was dressed in blue cloth and white linen, and wore in his lapel the red ribbon of the Legion of Honor's Grand Officers. In reclaiming his creature comforts, he had recovered his old martial elegance. He stood very straight. His face, solemn and mysterious, marked by happiness and hope, seemed rejuvenated and fuller. He no more resembled the Chabert of the old greatcoat than an old sou resembles a newly minted forty-franc gold piece. Looking at him, anyone could easily have recognized one of the noble remnants of our former army, one of those heroic men who reflect our national glory the way a shining sliver of ice seems to reflect the sun's rays. These old soldiers, taken together, are like living history.

When the Count jumped down from his cab to go to Derville's, he was as light on his feet as a young man. No sooner had his cab pulled away than a pretty carriage adorned with heraldic bearings drove up. Countess Ferraud emerged from it dressed simply but in a way designed to show off her youthful figure. She had on a charming hood lined in pink which perfectly framed her face, softening its contours and making it look younger.

If the clients were rejuvenated, the office remained as it was, offering the same image with which this story began. Simonnin was eating his lunch, his shoulder leaning against the open window. He was looking at the blue sky through the opening of that courtyard surrounded by blackened buildings on all four sides.

"Ha!" cried the little clerk, "who wants to bet tickets to the theater that Colonel Chabert is a general and a *Cordon Rouge*?"

"The chief must be some kind of magician!" said Godeschal.

"Then there's no trick to play on him this time?" asked Desroches.

"Countess Ferraud will see to that!" said Boucard.

"Come on," said Godeschal, "then the Countess Ferraud would have to belong to two men . . . "

"Shhh, here she is!" said Simonnin. Just then the Colonel entered and asked for Derville.

"He is in, Monsieur," Simonnin replied.

"So you are not deaf then, little rascal?" said Chabert, taking the gutter-jumper by the ear and twisting it, much to the satisfaction of the other clerks, who began to laugh and looked at the Colonel with the curious respect due to such a singular character. Count Chabert was already in Derville's office by the time his wife came in the study door.

"What do you say, Boucard, there's going to be quite a scene in here! She can spend the even days with Count Ferraud and the odd ones with Count Chabert."

"In leap years," said Godeschal, "there will be a *recount*."

"Keep quiet, gentlemen, they can hear us," Boucard said sternly. "I've never seen an office where they joke about the clients the way you do." Derville had shown the Colonel into the inner chamber when the Countess arrived.

"Madame," he said, "not knowing whether it would be agreeable to you to see Count Chabert, I have separated you. If, however, you desire . . . "

"Monsieur, I thank you for your consideration."

"I have drawn up an agreement whose conditions you and Monsieur Chabert may discuss at the present consultation. I will go alternately between you to explain your respective positions."

"Let us get on with it, Monsieur," said the Countess, betraying her impatience.

Derville read, "*Between the undersigned: Monsieur Hyacinthe, called Chabert, Count, Maréchal de Camp, and Grand Officer of the Legion of Honor, living in Paris, Rue du Petit-Banquier, on the one part; and Madame Rose Chapotel, wife of Count Chabert, the aforementioned, born . . .*"

"Never mind," she said, "skip over the preamble and get to the conditions."

"Madame," said the lawyer, "the preamble explains succinctly the position in which you both find yourselves. Then, in the first clause, you acknowledge in the presence of three witnesses—two notaries and the dairyman with whom your husband lives—to whom I have confided the secret of your affair and who will preserve the deepest silence; you acknowledge, as I said, that the individual designated in the documents attached to the deed, but whose state is otherwise established by a certificate of identification prepared by your notary, Alexandre Crottat, is your first husband, Count Chabert. In the second clause, Count Chabert, in the interest of your happiness, promises to exercise his rights only in the circumstances set forth in the agreement itself. And these circumstances are only the failure to carry out the conditions of this secret agreement. For his part Monsieur Chabert agrees, with your consent, to seek a judgment that would annul his death certificate and dissolve your marriage."

"I do not find that acceptable," said the Countess with surprise. "I do not wish to be party to a suit. You know why."

"In clause three," the lawyer went on with unflappable calm, "you pledge to pay, in the name of Hyacinthe, Count Chabert, an annuity of 24,000 francs on government bonds held in his name, which will revert to you on his death . . ."

"But that is much too much!" said the Countess.

"Can you come up with a better proposal?"

"Perhaps."

"What do you want, Madame?"

"I want . . . I do not want to be party to a suit, I want . . ."

" . . . him to remain dead," Derville broke in quickly.

"Monsieur," said the Countess, "if it is a matter of 24,000 francs a year, then we will go to court . . ."

"Yes, we will go to court," cried the muffled voice of the Colonel, who opened the door and suddenly appeared before his wife, one hand in his waistcoat and the other hanging by his side, a gesture given terrible significance by the memory of his adventure.

"It's him," said the Countess to herself.

"Too much?" repeated the old soldier. "I gave you nearly a million and you are haggling over my misery. Very well, now I want you and your fortune. We hold our property in common, our marriage is not dissolved . . ."

"But Monsieur is not Colonel Chabert!" cried the Countess, feigning surprise.

"Ah!" said the old man in a deeply ironic tone, "Do you want proof? I took you from the Palais Royal . . ."

The Countess blanched. Seeing her turn pale under her rouge, the old soldier hesitated, moved by the obvious suffering he was inflicting on a woman he had once ardently loved. But she shot him such a venomous look that he went on at once, "You were at the . . ."

"Be so good, Monsieur," the Countess said to the lawyer, "as to allow me to withdraw. I did not come here to listen to such appalling stuff." She rose and went out. Derville rushed into the office after her. But the Countess had found wings, it seems, and taken flight. Returning to his private study, he found the Colonel pacing back and forth in a violent rage.

"In those days every man took his wife where he wished," he was saying, "but I was foolish and chose poorly. I trusted appearances. She has no heart."

"Well, Colonel, I was right, wasn't I, to urge you not to come in? I am now convinced of your identity. When you appeared, the Countess made a movement that gave her away. But you have lost our suit; your wife knows that you are unrecognizable."

"I will shoot her!"

"Madness! You will be caught and executed like any poor wretch. Besides, you might miss. If you are going to shoot your wife, you mustn't, under any circumstances, miss her. Let me repair the damage—you are acting like an overgrown child! Go now. And be careful, she is capable of setting some trap that will land you in Charenton. I will notify her of our proceedings in order to protect you from any surprise."

The poor Colonel obeyed his young benefactor and departed, stammering apologies. He walked slowly down the steps of the dark staircase, lost in somber thoughts, perhaps overcome by the blow he had just suffered—so cruelly and deeply did it penetrate his heart. When he reached the lowest landing, he heard the rustle of a dress, and his wife appeared.

"Come, Monsieur," she said, taking him by the arm in a movement familiar to him from the old days. The Countess' action, her tone of voice gracious again, calmed the Colonel down, and he let her lead him to her carriage. "Get in!" said the Countess when the valet had finished unfolding the step. And he found himself, as if by magic, sitting in the carriage next to his wife.

"Where to, Madame?" asked the valet.

"To Groslay," she said.

The horses set off and carried them across Paris.

"Monsieur!" the Countess said to the Colonel in a tone of voice that betrayed how thoroughly she'd been shaken. In these rare moments of emotion, the heart, fibers, nerves, face, body, and soul—our whole being, every pore quivers. Life no longer seems to be inside us. It bursts out, contagious, transmitted by a look, a tone of voice, a gesture, imposing our will on others. The old soldier quivered when he heard that single word, that first terrible *Monsieur!* But it was at once a reproach, a supplication, a pardon, a hope, a despair, a question, and an answer. This word included everything. It would take an actress to endow a single word with such eloquence, such feeling. The truth is not so fully expressed, it does not display everything on the outside, but allows a glimpse of all that lies within. The Colonel had a thousand feelings of remorse for his suspicions, his demands, his anger, and lowered his eyes so as not to reveal his agitation. "Monsieur," the Countess repeated after an imperceptible pause, "I recognized you immediately!"

"Rosine," said the old soldier, "those words are the only balm that could make me forget my troubles." Two large, hot tears rolled onto his wife's hands, which he squeezed with a paternal tenderness.

"Monsieur," she continued, "could you not have guessed what it cost me to appear before a stranger in such a false position? If I am to be so compromised, let us at least keep it in the family. Shouldn't this secret remain buried in our hearts? You will forgive me, I hope, for my apparent indifference to the misfortunes of a Chabert whose existence I had every reason to doubt. I received your letters," she added hastily, reading the objection expressed in her husband's eyes, "but they reached me thirteen months after the battle of Eylau. They were opened, soiled, the writing was unrecognizable, and after obtaining Napoleon's signature on my new marriage contract, I had to believe that some clever swindler wanted to trick me. So to avoid disturbing Count Ferraud's peace of mind and upsetting my new family, I had to take precautions against a false Chabert. Tell me, was I not right?"

"Yes, you were right. I was a fool, a brute, an idiot, not to have seen the consequences of such a situation . . . but where are we going?" asked the Colonel, observing that they had reached the entrance to La Chapelle.

"To my country house, near Groslay, in the valley

of Montmorency. There, Monsieur, we shall meditate together on what course we should take. I know my duties. I may be yours by right, but I am not so in fact. Can you possibly want us to become the talk of Paris? Let's keep this rather ridiculous situation out of the public eye, and somehow preserve our dignity. You still love me," she went on, looking sadly and tenderly at the Colonel, "but did I not have the right to form other attachments? We are in a strange position, and a secret voice keeps telling me to hope for your good will, which I know so well. You are the sole arbiter of my fate. Be both judge and party to the suit. I entrust myself to the nobility of your character. Will you have the generosity to forgive me for my innocent mistakes? I admit to you that I love Monsieur Ferraud. I thought I had the right to love him, and am not embarrassed to admit this to you; if it offends you, it does us no dishonor. I cannot conceal the facts from you. When fate made me a widow, I had no children."

The Colonel gestured to his wife to be silent, and for a mile and a half they traveled along without uttering a word. Chabert imagined he could almost see the two young children before him.

"Rosine."

"Monsieur?"

"Are the dead wrong to come to life again?"

"Oh, Monsieur, no, no! Do not think me ungrateful.

Only now you find a lover and a mother where you thought you had left a wife. If it is no longer in my power to love you, I know what I owe you, and can still offer you a daughter's affections."

"Rosine," replied the old man in a gentle voice, "I feel no more resentment against you. We will forget everything," he added with one of those gracious smiles that always reflects a noble soul. "I am not crude enough to demand the gestures of love from a wife who no longer loves me."

The Countess looked at him with such gratitude that poor Chabert would have been glad to sink back into his grave at Eylau. Certain men have souls strong enough for such devotion, and find sufficient reward in making a beloved woman happy.

"My friend, we shall speak of all this later on with calmer hearts," said the Countess.

The conversation turned to other things, for it was impossible to continue long on this subject. Although the couple returned repeatedly to their peculiar position, either directly or by way of allusion, they had a charming drive, recalling the events of their past life together and the matters of the Empire. The Countess knew how to imbue these recollections with a tender charm and tinged the conversation with the melancholy needed to maintain its serious cast. She revived his love without exciting his desire, and gave her first husband a glimpse of her newfound moral depth—all the while encouraging him to restrict his happiness to the joys a father might feel in the company of a favorite daughter. The Colonel had known a Countess of the Empire; now he was seeing a Countess of the Restoration. At last they arrived by a shortcut at a large park situated in the little valley that separates the heights of Margency from the pretty village of Groslay. The Countess had a delightful house there, and the Colonel saw on his arrival that everything had been readied for their stay.

Misfortune is a kind of talisman whose power confirms our original nature; it increases mistrust and meanness in certain men, just as it improves the goodness of those with kind hearts. Adversity had made the Colonel better and even more helpful than he had been, and so he was able to penetrate the secrets of womanly distress that are unknown to most men. Nonetheless, despite his trusting nature he could not help saying to his wife, "Then you were so sure of bringing me here?"

"Yes," she replied, "If I found Colonel Chabert in the plaintiff." The air of truth she managed to put into this answer dissipated the slight suspicions the Colonel was now ashamed to have entertained. For three days the Countess behaved admirably toward her first husband. With her tender attentions and unflagging sweetness she seemed determined to efface the memory of the hardships he had known, and to be forgiven for the sorrows which, according to her confession, she had caused in all innocence. She delighted in displaying the charms to which she knew he was susceptible, while preserving an air of melancholy; for we all find certain manners and graces of the heart or mind irresistible. She tried to interest him in her position, to soften him enough to control his mind and prompt him to do her bidding.

Determined at all costs to attain her goals, she was still not exactly sure what to do with this man—but certainly meant to destroy him socially. On the evening of the third day she felt that, despite her efforts, she could not conceal the tension she felt as a result of her maneuvers. In order to spend a quiet moment to herself, she went up to her room, sat at her desk, and cast off the mask of serenity which she preserved in the presence of Count Chabert—the way a tired actress, returning to her dressing room after an exhausting fifth act, falls half-dead on her chaise, leaving on stage an image of herself she no longer resembles. She took up a letter she had started writing to Delbecq, enjoining him to go in her name to Derville and demand to read the documents concerning Colonel Chabert, to copy them and come immediately to Groslay. She had just finished when she heard the sound of the Colonel's agitated steps coming down the hall to find her.

"Alas!" she said aloud, "I wish I were dead! This is becoming intolerable."

"Well now, what's the matter?" asked the good man.

"Nothing, nothing," she said. She rose, left the Colonel and went downstairs to speak privately to her personal maid, whom she sent off to Paris with orders to make sure she herself handed the letter to Delbecq, and to report back as soon as he had read it. Then the Countess went to sit on a bench where she was sufficiently visible for the Colonel to join her when he chose. The Colonel, who was already looking for his wife, rushed over and sat down beside her.

"Rosine," he said to her, "what's the matter?"

She did not answer. The evening was one of those exquisite, calm evenings in the month of June whose hidden melodies lend such sweetness to the sunsets. The air was pure and the stillness so deep, that in the distant park one could hear children's voices, which added a kind of harmony to the splendors of the landscape.

"Will you not answer me?" the Colonel asked his wife.

"My husband . . ." said the Countess, who made a movement, then stopped, blushing, and interrupted herself to ask him, "how should I refer to Count Ferraud when I speak of him?"

"Call him your husband, my poor child," answered the Colonel in a kindly tone. "Is he not the father of your children?"

"Well," she went on, "if Monsieur asks me what I

came here to do, if he learns that I have shut myself up here with a stranger, what shall I tell him? Listen, Monsieur," she continued, assuming a dignified attitude, "you must decide my fate. I am resigned to anything."

"My dear," said the Colonel, grasping his wife's hands, "I have resolved to sacrifice myself entirely to your happiness . . ."

"That is impossible," she cried, betraying herself with a convulsive movement. "Remember, you would have to renounce your identity and file the authentic forms."

"What," exclaimed the Colonel, "my word is not enough for you?" The word *authentic* fell hard on the old man's heart and aroused an involuntary distrust. He gave his wife a glance that made her blush. She lowered her eyes, and he was frightened to find himself forced to mistrust her. The Countess was afraid she had shocked the fierce modesty and severe honesty of a man whose generous character and innate virtues she knew well. Although these thoughts made them both frown, harmony was soon reestablished between them. Here is how it happened. A child's shout was heard in the distance.

"Jules, leave your sister alone," cried the Countess.

"What! Your children are here?" said the Colonel.

"Yes, but I have forbidden them to bother you."

The old soldier understood the delicacy, the feminine

tact implied by this gracious gesture, and took the Countess' hand to kiss it.

"Let them come," he said.

The little girl rushed up to complain about her brother.

"Maman!"

"Maman!"

"It's his fault, he . . ."

"It's her fault . . ."

Their hands were held out to their mother, and the two childish voices mingled. They made an unexpected and delightful picture.

"Poor children!" cried the Countess, no longer holding back her tears, "I shall have to leave them. Who will be granted custody? A mother's heart cannot be divided; I want them myself!"

"Are you making Maman cry?" said Jules, looking angrily at the Colonel.

"Be quiet, Jules," cried the mother imperiously.

The two children stood silently, examining their mother and the stranger with an inexpressible curiosity.

"Oh, yes," she went on, "if I am separated from the Count, let them leave me the children and I will gladly suffer anything."

These were the decisive words.

"Yes," cried the Colonel as if completing a sentence

begun in his mind, "I must sink back into the grave. I have already told myself so."

"How could I accept such a sacrifice?" replied the Countess. "Some men die to save the honor of their mistress, but they only give their lives once. You would be giving your life every day! No, no, it's impossible. If it were only a question of your life, that would be nothing. But to testify in writing that you are not Colonel Chabert; to admit that you are an impostor; to give your honor while telling a lie every hour of the day—human devotion does not extend that far. Think about it! No. Without my poor children, I would have already fled with you to the ends of the earth."

"But might I not live here in your little summer house, as one of your relatives?" continued Chabert. "I am as worn out as a scrapped cannon. I need only a little tobacco and *Le Constitutionnel*."

The Countess dissolved in tears. Countess Ferraud and Colonel Chabert continued their duel of generosity, from which the old soldier emerged victorious. That evening, seeing this mother among her children, the soldier was seduced by the touching graces of a family scene in the country, in the dusk and stillness. He resolved to remain dead, and no longer fearing the power of some document, asked how he might go about once and for all insuring the happiness of this family.

"Do just as you like," the Countess answered him.

"I assure you that I will not meddle in this affair. I couldn't."

Delbecq had arrived several days earlier, and following the Countess' verbal instructions, had been able to gain the old soldier's confidence. The following morning, then, Colonel Chabert departed with the former lawyer for Saint-Leu-Taverny, where Delbecq had asked a notary to draw up a document couched in such crude terms, that after hearing it read, the Colonel promptly walked out of the office.

"Thunder and lightning! A fine sort I would be! I would have to say I'm a swindler!"

"Monsieur," said Delbecq, "I do not advise you to sign too quickly. In your place I would demand at least 30,000 pounds annuity from this arrangement. Madame would certainly be willing to give it to you."

With the indignant eye of an honest man, the Colonel saw through this practiced rogue, and was prey to a thousand warring feelings. He grew in turn distrustful, outraged, calm. At last he stepped through a hole in the wall into the park at Groslay and went to rest and reflect privately in a small downstairs room of the garden house, from which the Saint-Leu road could be seen. The path was strewn with soft yellow sand, and the Countess, who was sitting upstairs contemplating her triumphs, was too absorbed to hear the Colonel in any case. Nor did the old soldier notice that his wife was in the room just above him.

"So, Monsieur Delbecq, has he signed?" the Countess called to her steward, whom she saw walking alone on the path beyond the hedge of a sunken fence.

"No, Madame. I don't even know what's become of him. The old horse has bolted."

"So while he's still within our grasp, let's have him locked up in Charenton," she said.

The Colonel recovered his youthful agility enough to leap over the fence. In the blink of an eye he was standing before the secretary, and delivered a couple of the smartest slaps an attorney's cheeks have ever received.

"You can add that old horses know how to kick," he said.

Once his anger had dissipated, the Colonel no longer felt he had the strength to jump the ditch. The truth had been revealed in all its nakedness. The Countess' words and Delbecq's reply unveiled the plot he had nearly fallen for. The attentions she had lavished on him were the bait to catch him in a trap. These words were like a drop of subtle poison, signaling a return of all the old soldier's physical and moral sufferings. He came back toward the garden house by the park gate, walking slowly, like a broken man.

So there would be neither peace nor truce! From this moment he would have to wage the hateful war with this woman that he had discussed with Derville; entering into a life of litigation; feeding on gall; drinking the dregs of bitterness each day. Then—a frightening thought—where would he find the money to pay for the first hearings? He was seized by such a disgust with life that had there been a body of water nearby he would have thrown himself in; or had pistols been at hand he would have blown his brains out. Then he fell back into the confusion which had altered his spirits since his conversation with Derville at the dairyman's. Once he reached the garden house, he climbed upstairs to a little room with rose windows facing onto the ravishing vistas of the valley, where he found his wife seated on a chair. The Countess was examining the countryside with a ruthless expression of utter, impenetrable calm. She wiped her eyes as if she had wept, and toyed distractedly with the long pink ribbon of her belt. Nonetheless, despite her apparent assurance, she could not help shuddering at the sight of her venerable benefactor, standing with his folded arms, his face pale, his brow stern.

"Madame," he said after staring at her a moment and forcing her to blush, "Madame, I do not curse you; I despise you. I thank fate for severing our ties. I do not even feel a desire for vengeance, I no longer love you. I want nothing from you. Live peacefully on the honor of my word; it is worth more than the scribblings of all the notaries in Paris. I will never lay claim to the name I may have made illustrious. I am nothing but a poor devil named Hyacinthe, who asks only for a good spot to sit in the sun. Farewell . . ."

The Countess threw herself at the Colonel's feet, trying to stop him by grabbing his hands. But he pushed her away with disgust, saying, "Do not touch me!" She made an indescribable gesture when she heard the sound of her husband's steps. Then, with profound shrewdness, extreme wickedness, and fierce worldly egotism, she decided she could live in peace on the promise and contempt of this loyal soldier.

*C*habert, in fact, disappeared. The dairyman went bankrupt and became a cab driver. The Colonel might have applied himself to the same line of work at first. Perhaps, like a stone flung into a gorge, he skipped from cascade to cascade, sinking at last into the muck of rags oozing through the streets of Paris.

Six months after this event, Derville, hearing no more from either Colonel Chabert or Countess Ferraud, thought that surely they had come to some arrangement, and that in revenge the Countess had taken her business to another firm. So one morning he added up the sums he had advanced to Chabert and requested that the Countess Ferraud claim this sum from Count Chabert, assuming she knew her first husband's whereabouts.

The very next day, Count Ferraud's secretary, recently named President of the County Court in an important town, wrote this disheartening note to Derville:

Monsieur,

The Countess Ferraud asks me to inform you that your client completely abused your trust, and that the individual who claimed to be Count Chabert has acknowledged having acted under false pretenses.

Yours, etc.

Delbecq

"I swear, people are simply too stupid. And they call themselves Christians!" cried Derville. "Be a humane, generous, philanthropic lawyer, and you are bound to be cheated! This business has cost me more than 2,000 francs."

Sometime after receiving this letter, Derville was at the Palais de Justice, looking for a lawyer who worked at the Police Court. As chance would have it, Derville entered the sixth chamber just as the presiding judge was sentencing a man called Hyacinthe to two months in prison as a vagabond, and ordering him sent to the Beggars' Prison in Saint-Denis—essentially, a life sentence. Hearing the name Hyacinthe, Derville looked at the delinquent sitting between two gendarmes on the bench for the accused, and recognized in the condemned man his false Colonel Chabert. The old soldier was calm, motionless, almost inattentive. Despite his rags, despite his obvious misery, his face expressed a noble pride. His gaze revealed a stoicism that no magistrate could have mistaken; but when a man falls into the hands of Justice, he is nothing but a moral creature—a matter of law or fact—just as to a statistician he becomes a number.

When the soldier was led back to the Record Office to be eventually taken away with the batch of prisoners now being tried, Derville followed, invoking the right of lawyers to go anywhere in the Palais, and studied him for several minutes among the group of beggars. The waiting room was one of those spectacles which, unfortunately, neither legislators, philanthropists, painters, nor writers ever bother to go and see. Like all laboratories of chicanery, this waiting room is a dimly lit, evil-smelling place whose walls are lined with wooden benches perpetually blackened by the presence of wretches who come to this gathering place for every form of social distress.

A poet might say that daylight is ashamed to illuminate this dreadful sewer through which so much misfortune flows. There is not a single seat where some crime is not in the making or already committed; not a single place unoccupied by some man driven to despair by the stigma heedless justice has stamped on him for a minor offense—and who has started down the inevitable road to the guillotine or the suicide's pistol shot. All those who tumble onto the paving stones of Paris bounce off those yellowed walls. No humanitarian would have to speculate long to find the reason for all the suicides bemoaned by hypocritical and ultimately helpless writers; it is written right in that waiting room, and is a mere preface to the dramas of the morgue or the guillotine's scaffold.

Just now Colonel Chabert was sitting among those bold-featured men clothed in the ghastly livery of the poor, by turns silent or whispering quietly as three gendarmes on duty were walking back and forth, clanging their sabers on the floor.

"Do you recognize me?" Derville said to the old soldier as he stood before him.

"Yes, Monsieur," answered Chabert, rising.

"If you are an honest man," Derville went on, "how could you remain in my debt?"

The old soldier blushed like a young girl accused by her mother of having a secret love affair.

"What? Madame Ferraud has not paid you?" he cried aloud.

"Paid!" said Derville. "She wrote me that you were a swindler."

The Colonel raised his eyes in sublime horror as if asking heaven to witness this new deceit. "Monsieur," he said in a calm voice breaking with emotion, "ask one of the gendarmes to do you the favor of letting me into the Record Office, and I will write a note that will clear up this business."

At a word from Derville to the sergeant he was allowed to take his client into the Record Office, where Hyacinthe wrote several lines addressed to Countess Ferraud.

"Send this to her," said the soldier, "and you will be reimbursed for your expenses and your advances. Believe me, Monsieur, if I have not shown the gratitude I owe you for your good work, it is still here," he said, placing his hand over his heart. "Yes, it is here, full and complete. What else can the poor do? They love, and that is all."

"Didn't you insist on an annuity for yourself?" asked Derville.

"Do not speak of it!" answered the old veteran. "You cannot know how much I scorn that outward life which most men hold dear. I was suddenly sickened with disgust for humanity. When I think that Napoleon is on Saint-Helena, nothing on earth matters to me. I can be a soldier no more—that is my true unhappiness. After all," he added with a childish gesture, "it is better to be rich in feeling than in dress. I fear no one's contempt."

The Colonel sat down again on his bench. Derville went away. When he returned to his office, he sent Godeschal—by then his second clerk—to the home of Countess Ferraud, who, after reading the note, immediately paid the entire sum.

In 1840, toward the end of June, Godeschal, who was by now a lawyer, went to Ris with his mentor, Derville. When he reached the avenue leading from the main road to Bicêtre, he noticed beneath an elm tree one of those hoary, broken paupers who have earned the beggars' Purple Heart for having survived in Bicêtre the way indigent women live in Salpêtrière. This man, one of the 2,000 poor wretches lodged in the almshouse, was sitting on a stone focusing all his intelligence on a favorite operation of pensioners: drying their tobacco-stained pocket handkerchiefs in the sun, perhaps to avoid washing them. This old fellow had a striking face, and was dressed in the ridiculous reddish gown the almshouse provided for its guests.

"Hold on, Derville," Godeschal said to his traveling companion, "see that old man; isn't he like those grotesque gargoyles we import from Germany? Only this one is alive, and seems almost happy!"

Derville put on his glasses, made an involuntary gesture of surprise, and said, "that old man, dear boy, is a whole poem, or as the Romantics say, a real work of art. Have you ever met Countess Ferraud?"

"Yes, she is an intelligent and very pleasant woman, though perhaps a bit too religious," said Godeschal.

"That old inmate is her legitimate husband, Count Chabert, the former Colonel. No doubt she had him committed here. If he is in this almshouse instead of living in a fine home of his own, it is only for reminding the pretty Countess Ferraud that he found her, like a hackney cab, in the street. I still remember the tigerish glare she gave him at that moment."

Returning to Paris two days later, the two friends stopped at Bicêtre, and Derville suggested they pay a visit to Colonel Chabert. Halfway down the path, they found the old fellow sitting on a tree stump, holding a stick in one hand and amusing himself by tracing lines in the sand.

"Good day, Colonel Chabert," Derville said to him.

"Not Chabert! Not Chabert! My name is Hyacinthe," replied the old fellow. "I am no longer a man, I am number 164, room 7," he added, looking at Derville with that fearful anxiety common to old men and children. "Are you going to watch the execution?" he asked after a moment of silence. "He is not married, that fellow! He is very lucky."

"Poor man," said Godeschal. "Do you need money to buy tobacco?"

With all the naïveté of a Parisian street urchin, the

Colonel avidly held out his hand to each of the strangers, who gave him a twenty-franc piece. He thanked them with a dull look, saying, "Brave troopers!" He then pretended to shoulder his weapon, took aim, and shouted with a smile, "Fire both guns! Long live Napoleon!" And he waved his cane in the air, describing an imaginary arabesque.

"I suppose he's returned to childhood," said Derville.

"Childhood! Him?" shouted an old inmate who was looking at them. "There are days when you'd better not get in his way. He's an old rascal, full of philosophy and imagination. But today, Monday, what can you expect? He still thinks it's Sunday. Monsieur, he was already here in 1820. At that time, a Prussian officer whose carriage was coming slowly up the hill of Villejuif, passed this way. The two of us, Hyacinthe and I, were on the side of the road. This officer was talking as he walked with another officer—a Russian, or some other kind of animal—and when he spotted Hyacinthe, the Prussian, as a sort of joke, said to him, 'This old cavalryman could have been at Rosbach.' 'I was too young to be there,' he answered, 'but I was old enough to fight at Jena.' That Prussian took off without asking any more questions."

"What a life!" cried Derville. "Escaping from an orphanage, he comes back to die in an almshouse. Meanwhile, he helps Napoleon conquer Egypt and Europe.

Do you know, my dear boy," Derville continued after a pause, "that in our society there are three men, the priest, the doctor, and the lawyer, who cannot appreciate the world? They wear black robes perhaps because they are in mourning for all virtue and hope. The unhappiest of the three is the lawyer. When a man seeks out the priest, he is moved by repentance, by remorse, by passionate beliefs that elevate him and comfort the soul of the mediator. The priest brings a little joy; he purifies, he heals, he reconciles. But when he comes to us, the lawyers, we see the same ill feelings repeated again and again, never corrected. Our offices are gutters that cannot be cleansed.

"I have learned so much practicing my profession! I have seen a father die in a garret without a sou or a stitch of clothing, abandoned by two daughters to whom he'd given 40,000 pounds income! I have seen wills burned. I have seen mothers rob their children; husbands steal from their wives; wives use love to kill their husbands or drive them mad—in order to live in peace with a lover. I have seen women teach their legitimate children tastes that will surely be the death of them, while favoring some love child. I cannot tell you everything I have seen because I have seen crimes that justice is powerless to rectify. In the end, none of the horrors that novelists believe they've invented can compare to the truth. You'll soon become acquainted with such charming things yourself; as for me, I am moving to the country with my wife. I am sick of Paris."

"I have seen plenty already," Godeschal replied.

Paris, February–March 1832